Learn to read with

Baby bug

Words by Sue Graves
Illustrations by Jan Smith

book-studio

Mom gave
a present to
Baby bug.

"Happy birthday."
"Thanks, Mom."

"Happy birthday," said Mom. She gave him a hug.

"Wow!" said Baby bug. He dug and he dug.

"Wow!"

"A big green jug!"

First he dug up
a big green jug.

Next he dug up an old red mug.

"An old red mug!"

"I can hug this pug."

Then he dug up a toy pug. "Wow!" he said. "I will hug this pug."

Just then he
saw a rug.
He gave it
a big tug.

"I must tug and tug this rug."

Suddenly out
came the rug.

"Where is Baby bug?" said Mom with a shrug.

"Where is Baby bug?"

The end